Mistress of Paradise

This book is a work of fiction. Names, characters, places, and incidents are products of the author's imagination and are used fictitiously. Any resemblance to actual events, locales, or persons, living or dead, is entirely coincidental.

Alexandra Benedict

Mistress of Paradise

CHAPTER 1

There's no use in weeping,
Though we are condemned to part:
There's such a thing as keeping
A remembrance in one's heart.

"PARTING" CHARLOTTE BRONTË

The thick mountain mist swallowed Captain James Hawkins: a soul lost in paradise. The fog protected the runaway slaves, the rebellious Maroons, even the island ghosts from capture. James moved through the dense vegetation, slicing the feral ferns with a blade, searching for a fellow outcast. Sweat soaked his clothes as he scaled the steep and narrow dirt path, his only comfort the Undertaker's Breeze sweeping down from the peaks.

It was like passing through a hazy dream. The jungle was brimming with hidden, sensuous wonders: the mournful cry of a solitaire thrush, the light, sweet scent of ginger lilies, a brilliant and darting streamer-tailed hummingbird.

He stilled for a moment, admired the haunting atmosphere. It was tempting to lose oneself amid the fern trees or beneath a blanket of wild blossoms. There was a charm, a magnetic pull to the lush environment. But James pressed onward. He had a duty to perform.

After an hour long hike, he sighted the ramshackle structure: a two-story, wood frame house with a front verandah and slated window shutters. The exterior was in disrepair, the planked walls weather-aged. It looked abandoned, but smoke piped from the limestone chimney, indicating the mad devil was home.

There was a crash inside the abode, followed by a manic soliloquy.

James gathered his breath and wiped the briny moisture from his eyes before he stepped beneath the thatched awning. He set the cutlass aside, so as not to spook the old man, then rapped on the door. "Dawson."

Feet shuffled in a frantic manner inside the house. "Where's my gun?"

"You don't need your gun, Dawson." He pounded on the door. "It's James!"

A pistol cocked. "Who?"

James cursed under his breath. He remained stationed at the door, prepared to snatch the weapon from the raving hermit's grip before he fired a single shot . . . and hopefully keep all his fingers in the process.

The door opened.

James bristled.

He was greeted by the barrel of a pistol. But it wasn't the cold steel aimed at his nose that disarmed him, rather the pair of exotic brown eyes, trimmed with long, dark lashes, that peered at him suspiciously over the flintlock. The jungle mist reflected in the glossy pools of her eyes. She absorbed the gray and swirling light—drawing him into her as well.

"Who is it, Sophia?" cried Dawson.

She recoiled the weapon and rested it over her shoulder, her lengthy, thick tresses like smooth cocoa, spilling over her generous bust in soft waves. "Black Hawk, I presume? My father's told me all about you."

James hardened at the low, lyrical sound of her voice, like honey and smoke, so sweet and rough at the same time, and a profound desire welled inside him to hear her speak his real name. He was Black Hawk at sea—the infamous pirate rogue—but he ached to be "James" with her.

She stepped aside and welcomed him with a seductive smile. "Come in. Are you hungry?"

Aye, he was hungry. Deep in his soul, he starved for the woman's touch. At the age of thirty-two, he had never hankered for intimacy. He was accustomed to dockside whores, who fulfilled his carnal needs ... but Sophia was no wench.

She was a witch.

She mesmerized him, and he struggled with her for supremacy. He yearned for the upper hand that she had snatched away from him. She made him breathless. He shirked from the disturbing sensation. He was always in command of his senses, his family, his ship. But Sophia took it all away from him. She wrested a burning desire from his soul. *She* governed him in that timeless moment, leaving him powerless, his guts twisted, and he had a raw, inborn impulse to take back control of his wits.

"Shoot the blackguard, Sophia!"

The fearsome Patrick Dawson—a retired buccaneer who had once ravaged the Caribbean Sea—stepped out of the shadows, sporting a bushy black beard speckled with gray. A long scar stretched across his brow and nose, and he gazed at James with dark, rabid eyes.

"It's me, Dawson. It's James . . . Black Hawk."

The burly brigand studied him with a wary expression before he humphed, having recognized the unexpected houseguest. "What do you want?"

James stooped and entered the hut at the unfriendly invitation, his eyes firmly fixed on the vixen. She strutted across the room, lined with books about flora and fauna, with grace, setting the pistol on the table before she stopped beside the iron stove and stirred the steaming fare in the copper pot.

The homely chore contrasted with her more sensual nature. She was about twenty years of age. Tall for a woman. She was wrapped in a plain white dress, the sleeves sheared at the shoulders, revealing her slender, sun kissed arms, and his heart shuddered at the image of her long limbs snaking around his neck, pulling him in for a savage kiss.

He girded his muscles. Where had she come from? Dawson had no daughter. The last time James had pirated near the tropical island, Dawson had been living alone in the tumbledown shelter.

James soon realized the old pirate was still waiting for an answer, so he gathered his disorderly thoughts and looked at the brigand. "I'm here to visit with you, Dawson. It's been more than seven years since we last met."

James had anchored off Jamaica's coast a few

days ago. He had hiked the Blue Mountain Range as a matter of respect, for he owed the surly cutthroat a great deal of gratitude.

Dawson snorted. "Sit. Eat."

James rounded the table. He settled on a tree stump, serving as a stool, and for a moment the room was quiet except for the soft, rhythmic sound of the wooden spoon striking the copper pot.

The gentle taps bewitched James, the methodic strokes sounded like a shaman's unearthly chant. He had never listened to the domestic activity with such interest, captivation even. He sensed the woman's every movement. He imagined he could hear her breathe from across the room if he just closed his eyes and concentrated.

Dawson settled on a wood stump beside his visitor and scratched his shaggy beard. "How's Drake?"

The beats in his skull distracting, James stroked the back of his head, fingered his long, black hair, tied in a queue. "Father's in England. He's ill. I'm captain of the *Bonny Meg* now."

For more than fifteen years, Drake Hawkins had captained the pirate schooner *Bonny Meg*. James had served under his father's authority during that time. But one year ago, the man had weakened, beset with chronic headaches, bleeding gums. He had then transferred command of the sacred vessel to James, the oldest of the four Hawkins brothers.

"Hmm." The old pirate rubbed his chin. "Drake's alone in England?"

"No, he's with Belle."

"Is Belle your wife?"

James glanced at Sophia. He eyed her trim waist and round hips through the thin fabric of her dress, her figure in silhouette. The skirt's hem fluttered at her slender ankles, and he admired her bare feet, her toes smudged with dirt. He noticed how her slim brows dropped as she perused him in return, and his blood warmed to feel her meticulous exploration — and obvious interest.

"Mirabelle is my sister," James returned in a low voice. "I'm not married."

"Don't be daft, girl! Pirates don't get leg-shackled."

James refuted in an even manner, "My father wed."

The *Bonny Meg* was named after James's mother, Megan. Father had loved the woman greatly, and her death in childbirth thirteen years earlier had devastated all their lives.

Dawson swatted at the air. "Bah! Your father was always crazy."

James lifted a brow at the ironic statement.

Sophia offered him a knowing smile.

The mutual jest that had passed between them, the secret look that had revealed their inner thoughts, bonded the couple in a way James had never experienced with a woman: a level of intimacy that frightened him. And yet he ached for more, for a deeper connection.

He smothered the balmy impulse. He could not explore his desire for the woman. She was Dawson's daughter. The brigand had saved James's father from a miserable life of servitude, and James could not return Dawson's benevolence with betrayal. Besides, the witch had already ensnared his senses in an alarming fashion. He didn't need to fall even deeper under her spell.

"Are you thirsty, Black Hawk?" Sophia wiped her lean fingers against her skirt, the rubbing movement ever so erotic. "You looked parched."

She gathered a bottle and two glasses from the wood shelf next to the iron stove. In slow and determined steps, she approached the table, giving him the utmost opportunity to observe her curvy figure.

She wanted him. It was so clear in her exotic eyes. He was taken aback by her brazenness. He was accustomed to being in control of every situation, but Sophia battled with him for dominance. She seemed unabashed by his robust physique, his dark expression. In truth, she seemed to like him all the more for it. He was at a loss to understand her motives.

James looked away from the enchanting witch, the blood in his veins pounding, and met Dawson's black and cutting glare. The notorious buccaneer might be well into his fifties, but he still had fists like iron mallets.

James sobered.

"Have you come for my gold?"

"What?" James frowned. "I don't want your treasure, Dawson."

The mad pirate raked his teeth from side to side. "You can't have my gold."

"He doesn't want your damned gold, Father."

Sophia poured two glasses of white rum and served the men. She pushed the spirits across the table, skimming her fingers over James's wide hand, making him shiver with longing.

Dawson glowered at her. "You can't have it either, Alvera!"

"I'm *Sophia*!" She huffed, as if she'd made the correction a thousand times. She looked at James with less heat in her eyes. "My mother is Alvera."

Dawson spit. "The jezebel!"

Sophia rolled her eyes before she returned to the iron stove, and in that moment, James sensed the kindred soul within her. She was trapped inside the house as the mad brigand's caretaker. James appreciated the feeling of being trapped, burdened with responsibilities. He had so many duties of his own. He comprehended the woman's motives too. She was strong in spirit and body alike, capable of enduring great hardship, he suspected. But she needed a moment of respite . . . she needed him. And knowing that truth tugged at James's passions, eclipsing his good sense.

"Luncheon's ready," said Sophia.

The room was brimming with the tasty aroma of her culinary pains. She ladled the spicy stew into the wooden bowls with her left hand, then served the dishes. "It's mackerel in *tomatis* with onion, thyme and hot peppers."

There was an endearing quality to the way she said *tomatis*—the love apple—in her native patios, making James's ears prickle with delight.

He tamped the rampant emotions in his breast and stared at the food. That he was going to devour something *she* had prepared with her own fingers, aroused him, quashing all his efforts to remain aloof.

Dawson cupped the bowl and greedily swigged the soup, making slurping sounds.

James was a little more mindful of his own manners and reached for a spoon. Slowly he tasted the steaming fare . . . and had to keep from groaning, it was so delicious.

Sophia positioned herself across the table from him. She folded her fingers into a fist and lowered her chin on her hand, watching him as he consumed the stew with an engaging expression and a shrewd smile on her lush lips. She didn't need to ask him if he was enjoying the stew. She had only to observe him to know the truth.

Again she had the upper hand. Again she made him breathless. And James struggled to quell the burning need in his belly, the storm raging in his head.

"Aren't you hungry, Sophia?"

"Aye."

James hardened as she pressed her bare toes against his boot and softly rubbed his leg in a suggestive manner.

The pressure in his skull mounted, his heart beat loud and heavy. He gazed into her deep brown eyes, so wicked . . . so ravenous. Sweat gathered between his shoulders and pooled at the base of his spine.

I want you, James.

He resisted the tempting invitation, stiffened his resolve. However, she slipped her naked and dusty foot between his boots and stroked his legs in deliberate movements, scraping her toes along his calves, simulating . . .

James caged her warm foot between his knees,

glowering at her. He was strapped for words, beset by a maelstrom of dark, carnal feelings.

He needed to take back control. She beckoned him into perilous waters like a nefarious siren, but he would not yield to her bewitching call. He would not give her authority over his wits, his good judgment. To accept the woman's invitation would be akin to treachery.

Dawson remained more interested in the food. He was ignorant of the couple's growing attraction— or he willfully disregarded it—making it all the more grueling for James to resist Sophia.

The pulses in his head beat loud as she struggled to get her foot loose, the jerking movements quick and fierce, but he maintained control. He squeezed his legs firmly together, keeping her locked between his knees.

There was a fiery look in her eyes, a droll expression even. It was clear she didn't mind their battle of wills. She relished in it, it seemed. And that raised James's hackles. He wasn't there to cater to the woman's licentious whims. She wanted escape from her troubles and duties and responsibilities. She yearned for a brief surcease. He empathized with her, for he, too, was saddled with obligations. But he refused to submit to her desires.

"You're a very good cook, Sophia." He wiped his mouth with the back of his hand. He then pushed the empty dish across the table. "Can I have another bowl of soup?"

She glared at him. The heat from her eyes warmed his belly.

"Aye." Dawson burped. "Fetch me another bowl

too."

But Sophia was trapped between James's legs. The amusement in her expression flitted away. Her lips thinned instead.

"Are you daft, woman?" Dawson frowned. "We're still hungry. Get us some more food."

She kicked James with her unrestrained foot.

He didn't even flinch.

I have control, Sophia.

She accepted that truth. At length, she stilled. She relinquished command. He sensed the fight drain from her muscles as she relaxed her foot between his legs.

James breathed deep to feel her surrender, his bones thrumming in victory. He released her foot, allowing her to step away from the table.

She huffed. A dark fire filled her eyes, blood colored her cheeks. She snatched the empty bowls from the table and strutted across the room.

He watched her stiff movements as she ladled more soup into the wooden dishes. He was sorry to see her so piqued. He had formed an instant attachment to her as soon as she had opened the door. However, he would not betray Dawson by engaging in a heated affair with the woman.

She returned to the table.

"Thank you, Sophia," said James.

He brushed his fingers across her hand as she served him the pottage. He wanted her to know he still desired her, that he had not rejected her because he didn't want her … but because he couldn't have her.

"I'm tired," said Dawson.

"Let me take you to your room, Father."

"I'm not a babe!" Dawson brandished his arm. "Don't you have chores to do, woman? Leave us!"

Sophia eyed James one last time. It cut his heart, the hurt in her expression. She didn't seem to mind her parent's ranting, but she appeared disappointed that he had ordered her from the room . . . away from James.

James strangled the willful regret that ravaged him as she stepped away from the table and collected a basket of laundry beside the door before she vacated the house.

Sophia immersed another soiled shirt into the wash basin before she lathered the lye soap and scrubbed the garment across the ribbed board. She was able to afford servants, however her father was paranoid about strangers, leaving her entirely responsible for the tiring household chores.

She stilled.

Every fine hair on her flesh was tickled by the overwhelming sensation that she was being watched.

She ignored the black devil at her backside. She scoured the laundry with more vigor, her fingertips numb from the cold water.

A dark energy thrummed through her veins. He was not the man she had imagined him to be. He acted with airs. That repulsed her. He was a pirate. A cutthroat. He wasn't supposed to have moral fortitude . . . unless it was just a pretense. Perhaps the brigand did not want her because he found her unattractive. Had she misinterpreted the look of interest in his eyes? Had he gazed at her with curiosity, not longing?

She raked the garment across the coarse wood. What did the reason matter now? He had made his thoughts clear: he did not want her. So why was he still staring at her with such piercing regard?

Sophia heard his footfalls and stiffened. She closed her eyes as the seconds passed, shut out the sound of the soft mountain breeze and the distant songs of parakeets. She listened only to the low timbre of her heartbeat, the booms deep in her breast.

Her lips parted as he brushed past her like an apparition, but she didn't take in or even let out a breath. He stirred the air as he passed, and she absorbed the energy that came off him in his wake.

At last, she sighed. He moved off. She opened her eyes again, all watery, and shivered at the chill in the mountain air.

"Where did you come from?"

There was heat in his low voice. A sensual heat that stoked her listless soul to life. She wanted to ignore him, to resume her household chore, but his steely gaze was too magnetic to rebuff.

Slowly she glanced over her shoulder and studied his robust form. He had crossed the clearing and had settled against a fern tree, nine meters high. But he seemed more powerful than the mighty wood, and she yearned to touch him, to feel the warmth of his skin, the vigor in his muscles.

She rebuked herself for the foolish sentiment.

"I was raised in King's Town by my mother." She wiped her wet, soapy fingers against her skirt and lifted off her haunches. "But I came to live with my father a few years ago."

He folded his thick arms across his wide chest. He was dressed in black trousers and a loose, white shirt. She sensed the brawn pulsing beneath the fabric. She admired his hardy physique.

"Why? Dawson's . . ."

She arched a brow. "Mad?"

"Difficult."

She shrugged. "I didn't want to whore like my mother to earn my keep."

He looked at her thoughtfully, but soon the man's rich blue eyes darkened with clear desire.

She had not mistaken the passion in his blood after all. Her wounded pride rejoiced. He had turned her away because of her father, as she had first suspected. However, he still yearned for her … and if he would not come to her of his own volition, she would seduce him instead.

Slowly Sophia moved through the mist.

He visibly stiffened as she approached him. He might be the most infamous pirate on the high seas, but he was also a lustful man at heart. She didn't need to be too sophisticated in her seduction, she was sure.

She nestled between his muscular thighs, sighing. She was charmed, bewitched by the strength and passion coursing through his veins. She burned too. The desire welled inside her with a vicious need. But he remained staunchly still. Even his breathing was shallow, quiet.

"The mighty Black Hawk."

Lightly she caressed the rough stubble across his cheeks. She had listened to the whispers about the notorious pirate leader in town; his name was akin to a curse. The islanders feared him. Her father respected him.

She moved her hands across James's features, taking in every part of him. Her fingertips danced with vim. He was real. He was hard. She had waited for him to come, ever since she had first heard he'd anchored near the island, and she pressed her midriff against his firm belly, searching for more intimate contact.

She felt the spasms, the vibrations inside his bones. He still resisted her … but she would break his resistance.

The man's hot breath, feather soft, caressed her cheeks, and she pressed her fingers against his warm, sensual mouth, tracing the shape of his handsome lips, moisture gathering between her breasts.

She licked her dry lips. "You look just like my father described you." She moved her fingers across the thick ridge of his brow and down his long, sharp nose. "You look just the way I imagined you."

He shuddered. "You've dreamed about me?"

"Aye." She bussed his bottom lip, sweet with rum. He tasted so bloody good. Her heart ballooned, pressing on her lungs, filling her throat. "I've listened to my father's stories for years. I feel like I know you."

There was a dark, smoldering look in his deep blue eyes, as vibrant as the tropical sea. He was gripped with longing . . . and keeping a tight cap on his salacious desire. He wouldn't touch her, but he wouldn't pull away from her either.

She spread her fingers apart and raked her hand through his long, black tresses, tied in a queue.

"My father?"

"Sleeping."

"Good."

The man trembled. Sweat gathered between his black brows. She ached to taste the briny moisture there, but she wasn't tall enough to reach the delicious spot. Instead, she opened her mouth and cupped his lips with a soft cry of pleasure that shattered his stony façade.

James slipped his sinewy arms around her spine, caging her in a tight, crushing hold. He squeezed the wretched, suffocating emotions from her heart, wringing her soul.

She was dizzy with the taste of him, the heady warmth of his masterful touch. The man's musk, his essence enveloped her, filled her. He moved his lips with avid hunger across her mouth, and she let him ravish her.

Her every hair and bit of flesh stirred with longing as she shed the tiresome, habitual routine of her solitary existence, connecting with another spirit. She wrapped her fingers around his thick tresses, holding him in an anxious, almost violent grip.

"I want you inside me, James." She ached for the man's strong caresses, for his firm lips on her body. She ached for him to wash away the sluggishness inside her, to stoke her languid soul to sweet life again. "I've wanted you inside me for a long time."

"Tell me," he said roughly. "Tell me how you've wanted me."

"I've dreamed about you at night . . . I've touched myself thinking about you."

He groaned. "Tell me!"

She slipped her arms around his midriff, giddy at

the heat, the brawn she sensed pulsing through his veins. "I'd close my eyes and push my hand under the blanket. I'd rub my quim, thinking it was you touching me."

He made a soft choking sound. "Did you come?" His flesh glistened with sweat. "Did you come while thinking about me?"

"Aye."

He dropped his brow, so moist, pressed it against her own fevered flesh. "How did it feel?"

"So bloody good."

James bussed her lips, a soft and stirring kiss that sent blood pounding in her ears. "I want to make your dreams come true, Sophia . . . but I can't."

He gnashed his teeth in clear distress as he forcibly set her aside and walked away from her.

She glared at him, bewildered. "What's wrong?"

He glanced at the house.

"James . . . ?"

"I can't do this," he said, breathless.

But he was hard. She observed the erection pushing against his trousers. "The devil you can't!"

He glowered at her. "I mean, I can't do this to Dawson. You're his daughter!"

Aye, she was Dawson's daughter. Was she doomed forever because of her lineage? The islanders already treated her with disdain for being the mad brigand's spawn. Was she going to endure the agony of aloneness too?

Sophia gasped for breath as she struggled against her unquenched desires. She drowned in the woeful thought that she was destined to exist in isolation. James was the one man who admired her father, who didn't gaze upon her with pity or scorn. He would banish the lethargy inside her with his touch, his kiss. He would breathe new life into her tired soul.

But the black devil was loyal to her father. Dawson had saved James's father from naval tyranny, making her parent some sort of saint or paragon of righteousness in James's eyes . . . and making her his sacred offspring: a woman not to be touched—ever!

Sophia sidestepped the infamous rogue and returned to the laundry basin

"Sophia—"

"Leave." She hunkered and resumed the washing, putting all her restless energy into the vigorous chore. "You've visited with my father. You've done your duty to him. Now leave."

She sensed his towering figure looming behind her. The man's shadow caressed her spine. She listened to the harsh, raspy sound of his labored breathing. The swift tempo matched her own pulsing heartbeat. But soon he retrieved the cutlass beside the door and retreated, slipped back into the mist.

CHAPTER 2

There's such a thing as dwelling
On the thought ourselves have nurs'd,
And with scorn and courage telling
The world to do its worst.

"PARTING" CHARLOTTE BRONTË

James boarded the schooner, moored in the secluded Port Antonio bay. The *Bonny Meg* was home, his faithful mistress. She had always quieted the demons in his head and stilled the swirling darkness in his soul. Feeling her wide belly under his boots had always put the world to right . . . until now.

"Ahoy, Capt'n!"

James passed his loyal tars and returned the greetings as he crossed the deck in long strides before he scaled the steps leading to the poop.

The warm sea breeze whisked through his tresses, loose from the queue, teasing his cheeks. He ignored the playful caresses. He hankered for an island witch, who still tormented him even after his exhausting journey home.

The taste of her sweet lips lingered in his mouth. He looked toward the misty land, engrossed by the distant, ghostly mountains, and the knowledge that she was still up there, angry with him . . . yearning for his touch.

He shuddered. The memory of her in his arms filled his brain, making his skull throb. He wanted to crack his addled head against the ship's deck, he was such a fool. He should never have let the witch weave a spell over him. She had snared his desires, his good sense with her mesmerizing eyes and sultry island ways.

But she had captured more than his lust.

James closed his eyes. She had captured a private part of him he had never shared with anyone: an isolated corner of his soul that he'd guarded staunchly for most of his life. Her need to connect with him had reminded him of his own need to connect with another being: a need he had never fulfilled.

Footfalls approached. James muffled the maudlin sentiment, shoved it into the darkest recess of his soul. He opened his eyes and turned around to confront the ship's lieutenant, his brother William.

"How's Dawson?"

William folded his arms across his strapping chest. At the age of thirty, he was the second in command. A sage lieutenant, he was also the most level-headed of the Hawkins brood and often offered wisdom—welcomed or not—in the midst of adversity. However, James needn't seek advice from his brother about his quandary. He already knew what to do about the predicament: stay away from Sophia.

"The old brigand's still alive," said James, beset with stirring reflections, haunted by brilliant brown eyes. "He has a grown daughter, Sophia."

"Oh?"

"She takes care of him."

"Is she chained to the furniture?"

James snorted. "No, she wants to look after the surly brigand. She's a good cook."

"I see."

The rising inflection in William's voice suggested the man was suspicious about the captain's interest in Dawson's daughter, and so James quashed his brother's curiosity by switching the subject:

"How's the ship?"

"The ship is fine . . . but the crew is another matter."

James sighed. "What happened?"

"Eddie and Quincy had another row. Both fell overboard and landed in the water, but Quincy was injured."

James growled. The two fledglings in the family had a penchant for fisticuffs, and James was sorely tempted to maroon both their arses on the first uninhabited rock.

"Will the pup live?"

"He'll live." William scratched his chin. "I don't know how it happened, though. Quincy must have stepped on poisonous coral or a venomous fish, for he's suffering from some sort of rash."

"Blimey," James cursed under his breath. He sidestepped his brother and departed the poop, descending belowdecks through the open hatchway. "Where is he?"

William fell in step behind the captain. "I placed him in your cabin."

"What the devil is wrong with the forecastle?"

"The pup's in agony. He needs a nursemaid, and I figured it wasn't a good idea to put him with the rest of the tars. He would only disturb them with his yowls."

James sensed the blood pounding in his head. He opened the cabin door and entered his quarters. Quincy was prostrated across the coverlet, while Edmund tended to his injuries with a damp rag and a bowl of water.

"Hold still," ordered Edmund. "Stop scratching!"

"Sod off, Eddie! It hurts."

Quincy raked his fingers across his blistering legs, trousers sheared at the knees, the thirteen-year-old miscreant in clear distress.

"I leave for *one* morning and you two almost kill each other!" James stormed.

William quickly entered the space before the captain slammed the door closed.

James glowered. "I should shoot you both."

"Please shoot me!" pleaded the pup. "I can't take it anymore."

Edmund frowned. "I said stop scratching."

"I *can't*!"

James approached the bed. Fifteen-year-old Edmund quickly stepped aside, allowing the captain to examine his brother's legs in greater detail. "It looks like a jellyfish sting."

"Am I gonna die?"

"No."

"Oh!" Quincy curled into a ball, still scratching. "I wish I would die."

James looked at William. "Have a few of the men

go into the woods and search for Jamaican dogwood."

"Aye, Captain."

William departed the cabin.

Edmund shifted his lanky frame from one foot to the other. "Do you want me to stay and look after him?"

"No." James snatched the medicinal bowl from his brother. "You're going to take a bucket of water and vinegar and scrub the decks — all the decks."

Edmund bristled. He pointed at Quincy. "But *he* started the fight!"

"Fine!" snapped Quincy. "I'll scrub the decks and *you* can suffer with the bleeding sores."

"Enough!" James glared at Edmund. "Out!"

"Aye, Captain," he grumbled as he swaggered from the cabin.

As soon as Edmund had departed from the room, James heard the distinct sound of chuckling. He scowled at Quincy. The pup sobered and resumed his yowling.

James took in a deep breath before he placed the bowl of water on the table. "I'll try and wash away most of the toxins, but I'm afraid you'll have to suffer for the next few days."

"The dogwood?"

James gripped the pup's ankle, twitching, and patted his scrawny leg, so inflamed, with the moist linen. "The dogwood is to help you sleep."

"Sleep? I can't sleep! Knock me senseless instead. Please!"

"I can arrange that," he said grimly.

Hours later, the cabin was dark. James rested in

the hammock, swaying softly with the gentle swell of the sea. He listened to Quincy as he murmured in his sleep. James had prepared the dogwood tea and ciphered enough into Quincy's belly to make sure he was asleep for the next two days.

James rubbed his brow, pounding with fatigue. He ached for quiet in his soul. Ironic that he should only ever find it on the deck of the *Bonny Meg* in the midst of a tempestuous raid, but it was then that the canon blasts and roaring waves trumped his own noisy thoughts.

He rolled out of the hammock and approached the scuttle, peering through the small, round window at the moonlit mountains, so ghostly blue.

He had also found peace with Sophia. He had never had such a feeling of harmony away from the ship. He imagined the woman's thick tresses trapped between his fingers, her curves pressed in his embrace. He envisioned her warm, shining eyes ... and the bleakness he had witnessed in the lonely pools after he had rebuffed her advances.

She was caged.

Like him.

She wanted freedom.

Like him.

James glanced at Quincy, sound asleep in the bed. He was going to have to take care of the boy for a long time. He was going to have to take care of all his brothers—and his sister—for a long time. He had to endure his duty.

But he would offer Sophia respite from hers.

The thought snagged in his mind. There was no escape for him from obligation, but he had an opportunity to offer Sophia freedom from hers.

Aye, she was Dawson's daughter, but there was an unmistakable attraction between them: one he had to satisfy for both their sakes.

Sophia closed her eyes and listened to the rhythmic drumbeats, swaying her hips to the music. In the twilight hours, the melodic pounding and bawdy lyrics offered her a clandestine moment to be wild and free, to dance and shake loose the restless energy thrumming inside her.

She opened her eyes and took another swig of rum before she joined her fellow outcasts, the rebellious Maroons, and stomped her feet in the jungle soil, high in the Blue Mountain Range. She was so high, if she reached out her hand, she felt she would touch the moon, the stars.

The flames from the bonfire snapped at her bare toes as she undulated alongside the other charmed figures, dubbing with the shadows, seeking flight from the darkness in her soul.

It was a cool night, the air brisk, pristine. She swallowed a mouthful of it, her heart thumping in tempo to the tune, her thoughts aligned with her sensuous surroundings.

The enchantment shattered.

Sophia shivered as an intruding presence filled the atmosphere. She glanced through the hazy smoke into the dark, dense woods.

He was watching her.

He was masked by the blackness, but the man's sharp stare pierced her spine, her flesh, teasing her senses, summoning her heart to heed his silent call.

She banished the thought of him from her mind. She danced with more passion, seeking refuge from his sultry glare, but the black devil taunted her with his closeness. If she shut her eyes tight, she remembered the rich taste of his lips, the intoxicating touch of his hard muscles, the unearthly connection she had briefly formed with him.

Sophia peered into the jungle once more, eyes watery from the stinging heat and thick smoke. She was sweating, her heart throbbing, her limbs aching ... but not from fatigue.

She was hungry.

She surrender to the brigand's invitation at last. She moved away from the fire, the warmth of bodies. She traversed the natural courtyard in a daze, the melody still pounding in her head, guiding her steps.

She entered the jungle. The drumbeats resounded in her ears as she searched the vegetation for him, reaching through the vines and ferns and darkness.

She stilled.

There was a silhouette, unlike a tree, yet vigorous and towering, positioned a few feet away from her.

"Black Hawk?"

The shadow shifted.

Sophia's pulses danced. She made no effort to ease her pounding heartbeat or cool her hot, throbbing blood. She trembled as he approached her with slow, leggy gaits.

"What are you doing here, Black Hawk?"

He settled beside her, a thick wall of muscle. She inhaled the rich scent of his masculine musk, the salty sea in his hair. She fisted her fingers to keep her hands at her sides, she was so tempted to touch him, taste him. But she didn't want to share another doomed kiss with the man. She didn't want to engage in another teasing, unfulfilling tryst.

"I heard the music," he said quietly. "I followed it."

She gathered her breath, her wits. "Father isn't here."

"I'm not looking for your father."

Softly he stroked her cheek. She shivered with delight to feel his warm finger caress her balmy skin. He possessed enough strength in his one finger to arouse her and make her weak in the knees.

"You dance beautifully," he praised.

He brushed the long appendage across her lips, trembling with need, making the blood pound in her skull.

She opened her mouth and kissed his finger to ease the pressure growing in her head, but he moved his finger deeper into her mouth, and she whimpered with even greater longing as he rubbed her tongue in sensual ministrations.

"So beautifully."

He bussed her top lip, his finger still in her mouth, quivering. She tasted the briny sweat, the need stemming from him.

"Dance with me, Sophia."

The man's sultry words of desire rolled across her spine, making her toes quiver. The taste of him in her mouth, the energy coming from his stalwart torso poisoned her cries of protest.

He removed his finger from her mouth and cupped her cheeks.

Sophia sighed as he slowly rocked his hips in

step to the music. She closed her eyes and wrapped her fingers around his midriff, matching his thrusts and undulations.

Their bodies moved as one, lilting to the melody. She pressed her breasts against his wide chest, seeking warmth and comfort. She listened to the man's deep, even breaths. She matched his heartbeat too. Soon they were a single being. Alone in the dark. Dancing.

"Sweet Sophia."

Sophia shivered as he exhaled, his breath stirring her locks in a whimsical fashion. She had no words. He enveloped her completely: body and mind. And she slipped deeper into the man's embrace, her flesh covered with goose bumps.

"I want you," he whispered.

The blood in her veins burned, her belly ached. There was a profound need budding in her womb. It pulsed and pleaded with her for surcease. And she knew the black devil would give her the succor she craved, that he would strip the chains holding her captive and let her spirit run wild and free.

He bussed her brow, leaving a warm mark between her eyes, the imprint of his lips. He kissed her nose next, still keeping her face pressed between his large palms.

"I'm going to move deep inside you." He licked her lips. "I'm going to make you scream with pleasure."

Sophia gasped for air. She parted her lashes and gazed into the dark and smoldering pools of his commanding eyes. The distant firelight reflected in the black orbs. She peered into his soul and shuddered at the welcoming warmth she found there, pulling her closer, even deeper into his heart.

"Are you a virgin?" he asked quietly.

"No."

"Good."

The salacious hunger pains in her belly growled. She clasped his wrists, starving for more intimate contact. However, she wanted to be sure he *really* desired to be with her, and she cut him a venomous stare. "If you walk away from me again …"

"I won't, sweetheart."

The low, lyrical timbre of his voice made her shudder once more with its musical ring, and she capitulated. He sensed her surrender as soon as she wistfully sighed, and in one swift movement, he captured her lips in a savage kiss.

He filled her senses with his breath and being, and she took in every part of him with ravenous pleasure, savoring the briny moisture from the sea that bathed his skin. She licked the salt, the rich musk from his pores. She opened her mouth and let him invade her with his firm, hot tongue.

He steered her body toward an ancient wood, hundreds of years old. It had crashed long ago in the dense jungle, its mighty roots exposed. He pressed her against the wide log, as high as her midriff. He moved his sweet lips over her mouth in avid hunger, lifting her skirt and wedging his narrow waist between her moist thighs.

She groaned. It was pure bliss to feel him grinding between her legs. She wanted him to envelope her even more, to crush the listlessness in her heart with his girth and his passion, to wrench the manacles apart that were keeping her prisoner.

Sophia circled her ankles around his waist, caging him . . . but he firmly untangled her legs, forcing her feet apart.

"Are you still fighting for control?" he said between raspy breaths.

She gazed into his dark eyes, so hard and hot. "I—"

He grazed her cheek with his thumb. "We do this my way."

She shivered, heart pounding. "And what's 'your way'?"

"Let me go, Sophia." He brushed his lips against hers. "Let me show you."

The man's tempting words weakened her, making the blood dart through her veins. He wanted control. She didn't mind giving it to him. She was always in charge of the household, her father. It thrilled her to think she might have the opportunity to submit to him, to let him be in command of her body.

She loosened her fierce grip around his neck.

He kissed her softly again. "Spread your legs."

She obeyed, sweat soaking her garment, cooling her fevered flesh.

"That's better," he said softly. He moved his large hand across her breast, her thumping heart. "Stay open for me."

He rubbed her breast in smooth, titillating strokes, leaving her quim untouched. She cooed with pleasure to feel the cool jungle mist at her throbbing clit . . . and the sultry heat from James's strapping figure.

"Yes, like that." He moved his lips across her stiff nipple. "Stay wide open for me."

Sophia quivered as he drew her nipple deep into his hot mouth, feasting on the sensitive flesh with ravenous regard through the thin fabric of her dress. She moaned with unabashed delight at the assault on her senses.

"You taste good, Sophia. So bloody good."

Her legs buckled.

"No," he said brusquely. "Stay open for me . . . wide open for me."

"James—"

But he bussed her mouth to keep her quiet, swallowing her entreaty as he kneaded her tender and aroused breast.

"I'll take you when I'm ready," he said roughly. "When you're ready."

She was ready now! she wanted to impart.

"We do this my way, remember?"

Sophia let him strip even more of her willfulness away. She let him have his ruthless way. And the more she relinquished control, the more pleasure he offered her in return.

"I think you're ready now." He slipped his large palm across her midriff . . . then lower. "Are you ready?"

"Yes!"

She groaned in intense pleasure.

The burly brigand fingered her clit, softly stroking the sensitive spot with his thumb, his other fingers brushing her opening in feathery touches.

Sophia bucked at the first steamy touch.

"Aye, I think you're ready."

He kissed her, shushing her wanton cries. His warm lips moved firmly over her mouth, keeping her hungry growls contained in her throat as his fingers rubbed her sensitive core to pulsing arousal.

"Does this please you?" he breathed hoarsely.

She gritted, "No."

He chuckled, slipping a strong finger inside her wet womb. "Liar."

She tightened at the slick feel of him inside her. "It doesn't please me enough."

"Hmm . . . Let me see if I can please you even more."

She moaned as he thrust a second finger inside her wet quim, stretching her even more. "How was that?"

"I want more," she said weakly.

"Then open for me even more."

Sophia lifted a shaky leg and wrapped it around his sturdy hip, spreading her flesh even wider apart for him, crying out as he pressed his thumb against the nub of nerves at her apex.

He nuzzled her cheek. "Doesn't that feel better?"

The sound pressure of his palm at her clit was mesmerizing, and she yearned for more . . . for sweet release.

She cried softly in need.

He bussed her throat and rasped, "Oh, sweetheart, I'll give you what you want."

Sophia quivered, her quim wet and ready for him, but he wasn't ready for her. He cupped her hips and turned her around, hoisting her slightly over the fallen tree. She grabbed the wood for support as he roughly pushed her skirt aside, scraping his fingernails across her sensitive buttocks.

He needed to be in control, she remembered. He needed to guide her through the erotic experience … and she needed to let him.

"Open for me," he commanded.

Sophia shuddered at the hot feel of his palms massaging her backside. She lifted one leg, keeping the other on the ground, and arched it over the log, giving him greater access to her quim.

He unfastened his trousers and soon the hot, velvety touch of his cock stroked her inner thighs, and she groaned in pleasure. "Oh, James!"

He grabbed her hips and guided the cusp of his erection into her wet womb, stretching her.

She moaned.

He stilled. "Did I hurt you?"

She clasped his hand, still firmly embracing her hip, and squeezed his fingers. "I'm all right. Don't stop."

He hesitated for a moment, trembling.

She raked her nails across his hand, scarping flesh. "James . . ."

Soon he grunted and pushed deeper . . . deeper, filling her with his hard, wide girth.

The heat and muscle and power surging through her quim was wonderful. She quieted her thundering heartbeats and ignored the pulses in her head to better feel the hot and rigid length of his flesh inside her womb.

"Yes," she sighed. "Yes. Yes!"

He thrust slowly, giving her time to grow accustomed to his size, his thickness, and she reveled in the heady sensation. It was such a liberating act, to surrender to his desires. She rejoiced in the thought that she needn't seek her own gratification, that she need only take the blissful comfort he offered her.

"Do I give you pleasure?" he rasped.

"Yes, sweet pleasure."

The pounding *mento* drums thumped in tempo to the brigand's hardier thrusts. "Is this what you dreamed about?"

"Yes!"

She gasped with each rough, undulating push, tears welling in her eyes. There was no pain, though. She suffered sweet surrender instead. He rocked her hips, pressed his breast against her moist back, slick with sweat.

"Did it feel so good in your dreams, sweetheart?"

Sophia cried with pleasure. She spread her legs even wider, relaxed her tight muscles, giving him her whole being. "*You* feel so good."

She was blinded by her tears and her long, loose tresses. But she didn't need her sight. She needed him. To feel him. To be one with him.

Free.

She was free.

So free.

"I feel good, do I?" he growled.

She was throbbing in ecstasy, so wet with need. She listened to the rogue's hard, hoarse breathing as he pumped inside her with swift and pulsing thrusts, her quim quivering with delight at the sound of his guttural groans and wispy sighs.

"Yes," she cried. "Yes!"

The pressure at her apex was great. He sensed she was about to come, for he offered her the stimulation she needed. He reached between the front of her legs and rubbed her clit, stirring her lust into a maelstrom of sensuous pleasure.

Sophia screamed. A rough and choking scream. The orgasm gripped her body in a viscous embrace as her muscles seized and pulsed and the fluids flowed freely from her womb, draining her strength, making her feel so weak and light … and free.

The brigand rammed hard, seeking his own feral release, squeezing her hips and rutting with firm and steady strokes before he gasped and grunted into the forest night, his shouts snatched away by the rhythmic music and singing dancers.

He embraced her, and together they rested against the ancient wood, starved for breath. He didn't push away from her after he had had his fill, like others had in the past. He wanted more. He wanted to touch her, to keep her in his arms. He melted the iron bars encasing her heart with his tenderness, and she closed her eyes, wishing for the moment to stretch on forever.

He stroked her leg, her wet back, her arms. He buried his lips in her mussed hair and took in a sharp breath, his nose grazing the back of her throat. "Did I give you what you wanted, sweetheart?"

The hoarse words funneled through her ear, ringing in her skull. "And if you didn't?"

He nipped her ear. "Then I would give it to you again."

She shivered. The tremors wracked her bones. She was so tempted to admit she needed more from him just to relive the experience, but she would not lie to him after what he had done for her.

"Aye, you gave me everything that I wanted."

He was quiet for a moment, his heavy limbs still draped over her sweat-soaked body. The aftermath was as dear to her as the coupling. Feeling his hefty lungs expanding as he breathed into her back, assured her the intimacy had not been a dream.

"I have to go, Sophia."

He said the words with an air of regret.

She gathered her muddy thoughts, her heartbeat more mellow, and opened her eyes. "I understand."

James pulled away from her. The nippy jungle breeze attacked her flesh, and she shuddered.

Slowly she righted herself and smoothed her skirt as he fastened his trouser flap. She eyed him for the first time since their wanton rendezvous, and sighted his bedraggled appearance, smiling inwardly, wondering if perhaps he had needed the fuck as much as she had.

"Will I see you again?" she wondered.

The brigand was silent.

Sophia smothered the disappointment in her breast. She would not allow the intrusive black thought to sully the memory of their heated encounter. She quashed the feeble sentiment outright. She had asked for one night of freedom. And he had offered it to her. It was unfair of her to expect him to give her more, however much she ached for it.

He stepped beside her, a towering shadow, and brushed her cheek with the pad of his thumb. "Good-bye, Sophia."

He then moved away from her and disappeared into the jungle.

She fingered her flushed cheek as she listened to

his heavy footfalls recede.

"Good-bye, Black Hawk."

CHAPTER 3

When we've left each friend and brother,
When we've parted wide and far,
We will think of one another,
As even better than we are.

"PARTING" CHARLOTTE BRONTË

Beams of sunlight pierced pockets in the forest canopy, illuminating the ethereal terrain. Sophia hiked along the narrow dirt path at a brisk pace, eager to reach the cave. She still had a long journey ahead of her, and she needed funds before she travelled into town to obtain supplies. She had informed her father about the trip, however the man had a short memory. She had to return home before it was dark or he might forget everything she had told him and panic, wondering if perhaps she had deserted him.

Sophia paused and sighed. She had considered it once: deserting her father. Two years ago, after a stormy row, he had challenged her tooth and nail, believing her her mother. He had even aimed a pistol at her, thinking she was about to poison his food. She had eventually convinced him she was his daughter, that she wasn't going to harm him. However, the traumatic affair had taxed her strength, her spirit even. Hopelessness had filled her soul, and she had ruminated about taking a piece of the brigand's treasure and abandoning him to his madness.

But she had not.

Sophia wiped the sweat from her brow. She resumed her hike, passing tall stalks of bamboo. She stilled again.

Slowly she reached for the delicate white blooms, mesmerized by the miraculous petals. She fingered the soft floral underside in awe. The bamboo flowered once every thirty-three years. She wasn't likely to see it, feel it again in her lifetime. It was probably as old as ... James.

Sophia closed her eyes, the sensuous blossoms stirring memories of the pirate's sensual touch, his breath. The buds had likely sprouted the same year he had been born ... and now again the year she had met him. Nature was like a calendar, marking time, recording singular events.

She scoffed at the romantic rot. The brigand had come from the mist and offered her a dreamy tryst before he had vanished back into the blackness. She would not see him again. It wasn't providence, their meeting. It was random chance.

A Giant Swallowtail butterfly fluttered across the dirt path. Sophia gazed at the black creature with brilliant yellow stripes and a wide wing span . . . as large as James's hand.

She huffed and cut through the jungle. She saw James in everything, it seemed. It'd been three days since she had parted from him, and still he pressed on her thoughts. Meeting the brigand might not be cosmically ordained, but he had uprooted her weary world, and now she was filled with a keen hunger for a more intimate connection: a spiritual connection.

Sophia slowed, crushed by the profound sentiment that she was alone on the island. The little time she had spent with James reminded her of how much she needed another voice — a sane voice — in the house, a warm touch, a bond that transcended physical pleasure. The ache welled deep inside her, crippling her steps and she stumbled, overwhelmed by the truth that she might never form such a bond, that she might never know true camaraderie or trust or joy.

A branch snapped.

Sophia's heart pinched. She glanced over her shoulder and scanned the woods, but the leafy stage was peppered with harmless plants and trilling birds. She had learned to trust her instincts, though, and slowly removed the pistol from the satchel strapped across her bust, crouching.

She listened for footfalls, but the pounding beats in her head muffled the noises coming from her surroundings. She eyed the jungle instead, scanning the lush terrain for movement … and spotted the rustling ferns.

Armed redcoats slinked through the dense vegetation, like two hounds stalking prey. The bloodthirsty villains heralded strife and death, and she lifted off her haunches, blood pulsing through her veins at a wild tempo, and pointed the pistol at one of the marching men. She was a skilled markswoman … but she was outgunned.

The soldiers stilled and aimed their muskets

straight for her head.

"Put down the pistol," ordered a redcoat.

Sophia considered darting through the bush. Musket fire wasn't very accurate. But she suspected, at such close range, the lead balls would find their way into her backside . . . and then who would take care of her father?

"Now!" he barked.

Sophia maintained a firm grip on the weapon, her heart thundering in her breast. If she lowered the pistol, she would be at the mercy of the ruthless redcoats. She might disarm, even kill one of the villains with a single shot, but his cohort would strike her dead.

Fingers quivered with repressed rage as she struggled between two poor choices, sweat gathering at her brow and under her arms . . . but at last, she lowered the pistol at her side.

"Drop it!"

She was reluctant. In her moist and shaky grip, the steel and wood flintlock offered her a smidgen of protection. She would sooner place the barrel at her own skull than submit to the brutal beasts . . . but then who would take care of her father?

Sophia gnashed her teeth and beat back the wretched tears that burned her eyes before she let the weapon slip from her stiff fingers.

The flintlock landed on the leafy forest ground with a soft thump.

The soldiers smirked.

"We only want some information from you, poppet."

Horseshit!

The redcoats killed and maimed and ravished the rebellious islanders. There was no room for "talk" within their vicious regime.

One man approached.

Sophia girded her muscles for the wicked assault, blood throbbing in her veins, pumping into her heart. The organ ballooned in her chest until her breastbones ached under the surging pressure.

"There was another uprising last night." The redcoat licked his sweaty lips. "Where are they hiding?"

"Who?" she said quietly.

"The Maroons, poppet."

She shook her head. "I don't know where they are."

"I think you do." He rested the musket against his shoulder, a lecherous look in his eyes. "I think you're one of their whores and you know exactly where we can find them."

Sophia twirled on her heels and dashed into the woods, but the brute grabbed a fistful of her long locks and yanked her roughly against his frame, twisting her neck and forcing her lips to meet his foul breath.

"Tell me where they are, bitch!"

But he was going to rape her whether she offered him the information or not, so she spit in his eyes to spite him.

The crack across her cheek blinded her for a moment, and she dropped to the ground in a daze, every nerve thrumming in her body. Blood filled her mouth, stained her lips. There was a swelling pressure in her head, squeezing her skull.

Sophia screamed as a weight crushed her back, pressing her breasts into the dirt, squeezing the breath from her lungs until she choked and gasped.

"Tell me, poppet," he said hoarsely in her ear. "Tell me!"

She wriggled and thrashed under his heavy muscles, seeking air. She felt an unnatural strength welling inside her, and she bucked her hips to get him off her backside, but he rolled with her wild outbursts, keeping her hair locked in his grip and her hands pinned under her belly.

"Eager for a fuck, are you?"

She sobbed deep in her breast as he fished for her skirt, raking the garment over her legs. The other redcoat smiled and maintained a firm watch with the musket.

"I get her next, Paul."

Sophia didn't want to know her attacker's name. She didn't want to know anything about the savage dog. She wanted to cut off his toes and pick her teeth with his bones. She wanted to strip the flesh from his muscles and hear *his* woeful wails.

He grabbed her quim, pumping the flesh with his fingers. "Hmm . . . you're a tasty dish."

She wanted to vomit. She kicked her legs and screamed inside her bones. He deepened the polluting assault, ramming his fingers inside her tight womb.

Sophia felt like she was drowning in thick, dark mud. Brain and body alike screeched in protest. She struggled in pain, but he overpowered her.

"Hold her, David."

No! No! No!

The other redcoat dropped the musket and kneeled at her head. He braced his arms on her shoulders and pinned her to the ground, while his brutal partner stripped his trousers, divesting his Tarleton helmet during the brawl. She pinched her legs together, thrashing, her heart swelling in her throat, but the devil wedged his knee between her thighs, forcing the limbs apart.

"A good fuck might stir your memory, poppet."

Sophia suffocated on her tears. She stiffened as she sensed the cusp of his filthy erection slip between her buttocks.

"Is this what you're looking for, poppet?"

She screamed in silence ... and then she gasped for sweet air as the heavy load was lifted off her backside.

Sophia coughed, spitting blood and tears. She glanced over her shoulder, eyes darting, but the redcoats were already dead or unconscious, their heads knocked against a tree. She eyed the blood splattered across the bark with pleasure.

Black Hawk stood over the limp carcasses, burly legs braced apart, fists clenched, chest heaving. She spied him through her tears, like a hazy dream, and she sobbed and laughed in both gratitude and pain.

He looked at her. The rabid blackness in his eyes burned bright. Soon, though, the pristine blue pigment returned, and his sharp breathing mellowed.

"Sophia," he rasped.

It sounded so sweet, the way he said her name. The low and familiar sound comforted her wild heartbeats.

"I . . . I'm all right," she stammered.

She smeared the blood, the tears across her features as she tried to wipe them away. She was trembling, vicious shakes that rattled her teeth. She was sore too. Every bone throbbed in agony from the assault. She sat on the ground for a quiet moment, grasping for her wits, her breath.

The leaves crunched under his sandaled footfalls as he advanced toward her, and she flinched.

He stilled.

"I won't hurt you, Sophia."

She sighed. "I know . . . I'm just . . ."

She hiccupped.

He crouched instead. "I have to touch you." He opened his fists and spread out his fingers in an unthreatening manner. "Let me see if your bones are broken."

She gathered her skirt and curled her legs together, wincing. "I'm all right."

But he cupped her ankle. "No, you're not."

Softly he fingered her leg. She swatted at his hand. He grasped her wrist and moved closer toward her, hunkering at her side.

"Your lip is bleeding."

She pushed him. "I'm fine, damn it!"

Sophia staggered to her feet and wavered, muscles smarting. He captured her before she stumbled, his hold firm and yet tender. But she yanked her arm away from him.

She wanted to weep. Three nights ago, his touch had been like balm, so comforting after so much solitude. However, now his touch was as sinister as the redcoats. It was all in her head, she knew it. He would not hurt her in such a vile way. But right then she couldn't stomach the intimacy.

She turned away from him and wiped the blood from her mouth, eyeing the lifeless figures sprawled in the dirt. Bile filled her belly. It seeped into every pore of her being. She gathered her shaky strength before she slammed her foot into one of the villain's cods. She attacked the other limp body with frantic zeal too.

After she had wasted her energy on the redcoats, she retrieved her pistol and returned it to her satchel before she resumed her hike, heading for the cave.

James followed behind her. He didn't touch her. He didn't even talk to her. He remained at her backside as she scaled the mountain range.

At length he said, "I can carry you."

She shook her head, her cheek swelling. She had enough strength to keep moving, for vim was still coursing through her veins at a rapid rate. However, she appreciated the pirate's company even if she wasn't ready to accept his help. She didn't want to be alone in the woods. There might be more redcoats skulking through the thick vegetation.

The steady drum of crashing water soon filled her ears, and she moved toward the sanctuary in eager strides. She was covered in filth and she squirmed in her own skin, yearning to cast off the layer of smut.

Sophia paused at the edge of the lagoon. She gazed at the welcoming water, a blended array of sapphire blue and emerald green. A tall and narrow waterfall spilled from the rocky cliffs above the grotto, stirring the pristine pool, while sunlight danced across the rippled surface, causing the waves to shimmer like jewels.

Sophia shuddered at the enchanting site. She wanted to immerse herself in the pure water and wash away the blood and loathsome handprints that still stained her flesh.

Tears streamed from her eyes. She slipped the wide, linen strap over her head in an unsteady manner and dropped the satchel on the ground. She then kicked off her shoes before she stepped into the warm lagoon and waded through the healing waves.

She inhaled a deep breath and dunked her head under the glimmering surface. She swam toward the base of the waterfall, the pounding surge pummeling her spine as she cleared the swirling pool and emerged inside the dark grotto.

She sighed, feeling safe, feeling clean. Crashing water resounded in the cavernous space. The smooth walls reflected the rippled waves. The splayed light danced across the stone surface . . . and the dazzling treasure troves.

Sophia scaled the glittering baubles and gold coins. She settled on top of a sturdy sea chest, raising her knees and wrapping her arms around her legs, rocking softly.

James surfaced moments later. He, too, had not removed his clothes. He was dressed in a loose, white shirt and cropped trousers. Drops of water like liquid pearls dripped from his sooty lashes. He combed his fingers through his wet mane and eyed the mountain of purloined riches.

"Dawson's treasure, I presume."

She shrugged. "It was buried all over the mountainside. Father had trouble remembering where it was all hidden, so I stored it here in the grotto to keep it together. I think I found most of it."

He stroked across the lambent water and rested his wide form at her feet. He remained inside the pool. He folded his strapping arms across a shelf of gold coins and set his chin, dark with stubble, on his forearms, gazing at her with his bewitching blue eyes.

"How do you feel, Sophia?"

"I'm fine." She shuddered. "I don't want to talk about it."

Pervasive images ran over and over again in her head. She struggled with the black and twisted thoughts, strangled the wretched cries still trapped in her throat.

James sighed. The man's breath slashed through the gloom and fear in her heart. She was not alone. He was there beside her.

"What are you doing here, Black Hawk?"

"What do you mean?"

"What are you doing in the jungle?" she said with a slight lisp, lips swollen from the attack. "Why aren't you raiding at sea?"

"I was looking for you."

She tamped the unruly feelings that stormed her breast, confusing her even more. "What do you want with me?"

"I need to talk with you about our night together. I need to . . ."

"What is it?"

He fingered a gold coin in a lazy manner, skimming his thumb along the circumference.

"We can talk about it some other time."

"We can talk about it now."

She needed the distraction. The sound of his deep voice was like salving ointment across her burned and blistered flesh.

He looked at her sharply. "You might be enceinte."

She snorted. "I'm not."

"Are you sure?"

She nodded. "I'm barren."

She had never conceived a babe in the past. She wasn't distressed by the truth, that she would never be a mother. She wasn't keen on the idea of parenthood. But she sensed the matter was important to men seeking heirs . . . even pirates.

"Does it bother you?" she said quietly. "That I'm barren?"

He gazed at her thoughtfully. "No."

"Truly?"

He was somber, features dark. "I don't want children."

She brushed a long, wet lock behind her ear. "So what would you do if I wasn't barren? If I had a babe?"

"I would do the right thing and take care of you and the child."

"Why?"

He was a pirate. He wasn't the sort to give a fig about where he rutted or with whom. Her own father had sired a hundred bastards like her, according to rumor.

"Because you're Dawson's daughter," he said firmly.

"And that makes me different from all the other whores?"

He looked at her crossly. "You're not a whore, Sophia."

She snorted again, the redcoats slurs still ringing in her ears, disabusing her of the thought.

He took her wrist. "Do you think that because of what happened?"

As soon as he had touched her, her heartbeat pattered and she gasped for breath.

He quickly let go of her wrist.

He had not harmed her. He had not crushed her in his mighty hold, but he had fingered her, and that was enough to send her senses into a fresh panic.

He seemed perturbed. "Let me take you home."

"No." She gathered her uneven breath. "Not yet."

She wasn't ready to go home. She wasn't ready to confront her father and carry the man's yoke of madness. She was still too distraught, too much in pain.

"Do you play?"

The brigand's low and gentle voice disturbed her fretful thoughts. She blessedly dismissed the turmoil in her breast and concentrated on the finely crafted wood box with gold clasp.

"No," she said.

He opened the box and removed the jade and ivory players. "I can teach you."

She observed his strong fingers as he arranged the lovely pieces across the checkered playing surface. There was something about his temperate hand movements that quieted the mayhem in her spirit. "Where did you learn to play the game?"

He shrugged. "My father taught me."

"I didn't know pirates played chess."

"He wasn't always a pirate. He was once a carpenter . . . before the navy took him."

Sophia had heard the tale. Almost three decades ago, Drake Hawkins had served the Royal Navy, pressed into service against his will. For ten years he had sailed the world under the dictates of a brutal commander . . . until the day her father had come along and attacked the naval vessel. He had offered the weary sailors an opportunity to join his pirate crew, and Drake had accepted the post, serving with her father for another two years.

"Your father's a skilled carpenter." Slowly she swayed in a comforting manner. "I know my father liked having him aboard the *Jezebel*, especially after raids. He was quick with the repairs. Father was sad to see him go."

But friendship had encouraged her father to release Drake from his pirate duty. After almost twelve years at sea, Drake Hawkins had reunited with his family in England. He had returned home with his fair share of the booty, and it was then he had captained his own pirate vessel, the *Bonny Meg*.

James pushed a jade player across the board. "Well, would you like me to teach you the rules?"

"I don't like rules. And why would I want to learn?"

"For the challenge."

"And if I win the challenge?"

"I mean—"

"I know what you mean." She glowered at him. "I'm not a fool. I can read and write, you know?"

"I know," he said evenly. "I saw the books. Do

they all belong to you?"

She nodded. "I like botany. I don't have the time or the space to garden, though."

He fingered a jade rook. "About the game . . ."

She sighed. "I just don't want to spend my time memorizing rules if I don't get something out of the game."

"Fair enough. If you win, you can ask anything of me you wish."

She eyed the brigand with suspicion. The proposal sounded attractive. She mulled over all the things she might want from him: a month's worth of chopped wood, or perhaps a tour of the *Bonny Meg*. But would he really give her whatever she asked for? Would he honor his word? She sensed that he would.

"And if you win?" she said askance.

"Then I can ask anything of you I wish."

She humphed.

"Is that a 'yes,' Sophia?"

"Aye."

He smiled. It was a quirk of the lips, really. The true pleasure was in his eyes. He had lured her into a match, distracting her from her otherwise woeful thoughts. She figured it was important for him to carry her away from her troubles, that he could not leave her to weep quietly in the cave. The man was unnerved by her tears.

Sophia listened attentively as he related the rules and demonstrated the movements across the board. After the lesson, he returned the pieces to their proper starting positions.

"Ladies first."

She eyed the lacquered board carefully before she

slowly moved an ivory pawn.

"I've noticed you're left-handed," he said in an offhand manner.

"It's wicked, I know."

"I don't mind wicked."

She scoffed.

He nudged a jade player. "How did you learn to read and write?"

"There was a Presbyterian priest at the whore house where I grew up. He schooled me in letters."

"The whore house employed a missionary?"

"He wasn't there to save souls." She moved another player. "He was one of my mother's patrons."

"Oh."

She shrugged. "He was young and alone in a strange world. He needed companionship. But I think he felt guilty about what he did with Mother. Instructing me in English was a form of penance."

James nabbed an ivory pawn.

She frowned.

"I see you don't like losing, Sophia."

"I'm not losing," she said firmly.

"I don't like losing either."

She glared at him.

"It's your turn, sweetheart."

After an hour-long match, Sophia gnashed her teeth as the brigand declared:

"Checkmate."

"That wasn't fair." She wrapped her arms around her legs. "You talked during the whole match. I couldn't concentrate."

"Then you should have told me to be quiet."

Alexandra Benedict

She curled her toes. "Well? What do you want from me?"

She waited with bated breath to hear the man's request, her heart knocking against her breastbones in frantic beats.

He returned the players inside the elegant box and secured the closure. "I want you to let me escort you home."

She sighed. "Is that all?"

He glanced at her sidelong. "That's all."

She had expected something more unreasonable from the man. She wasn't sure why, though.

The cascading falls obscured the terrain, but it was still easy to gauge the time of day. It was growing dark outside. The sun set early in Jamaica, soon after six o'clock, even in the summer months. The shadows were already creeping inside the grotto.

"Fine," she said in acquiescence. "You can take me home."

She grabbed a few coins from the treasure heap, for she would have to fetch the household supplies the following day. She then eased off the bejeweled peak, her limbs still sore, plunging into the warm pool.

Sophia surfaced in the lagoon again, the burly brigand at her side. She mounted the shore. A cool mountain breeze whisked through the trees, stirring the leaves, chilling the air.

She shivered . . . then stiffened as a set of hard, wet arms circled her shoulders, heating the blood in her veins. She sensed her heart hammering between her ribs as he molded his chest along the curve of her spine.

He hugged her in a soft embrace yet she gasped for breath. The man's heart thumped against her shoulder blade, like knuckles rapping at a secured door. She opened the door that concealed her being, allowing James to slip inside the dark hideaway, and for an intimate moment, she existed alone in the world with him.

Sophia folded her fingers around his wrist, nestled beside her cheek. The man's pulse tapped against her fingertips in steady beats, the life teeming inside him so stimulating.

He complied with her silent request to be released. He opened his arms and she stepped away from him, awash with the biting sensation of aloneness. She retrieved her footwear in a daze, and secured the blunt inside the satchel, still resting in the tall grass where she had dropped it, before she and James set off for her father's home.

The couple trekked in comfortable silence for a while. Then:

"Why do you stay with Dawson?"

Sophia swatted at the ferns. "He needs me."

"You stay with him out of charity?"

"No." She shrugged. "If he hadn't taken me in when I was thirteen, I would be like my mother."

"So you stay with him out of loyalty?"

"That's right."

James was quiet for a moment. "I understand."

She glanced at the man's wide, dark figure. "You don't think I'm daft for staying with the brigand? For taking care of him?"

"He's your family."

"But he's mad."

James snorted. "You haven't met my brothers."

Her voice softened. "I'd like to meet your brothers one day."

Sophia had no other family. She was curious to know how James interacted with his kin. She was curious to know the other brothers.

He sighed. "I don't think I can vouch for their gentlemanly behavior."

"Well, I've never met a gentleman, so there's no harm."

"Hmm . . . I suppose I can set up a meet."

"Bring them to supper one night," she suggested. "I'll prepare an island delicacy."

Quiet settled between them again.

Sophia didn't mind the stillness. However, she sensed the pirate captain's sharp stare on her spine, and she quivered, reckoning he had another grave matter to impart.

"You're not safe in the mountains, Sophia."

He had breached the fragile cocoon she had spun around her heart with his stark reflection. Her fingers trembled as sadistic memories stormed her brain: the blood, the tears after the redcoat's attack.

She shuddered at the hurtful thoughts. "I'm safe with my father."

"And when you're not with your father?"

"I can take care of myself," she insisted. "I always carry a pistol for protection."

"Why didn't you use it today?"

She tamped the fiery wounds deep into her battered soul, bandaged the ugly gashes. "I could have shot one of the redcoats" —*or myself*, she thought grimly — "but then the other soldier would've killed me . . . and who would take care of my father?"

"They might have killed you after the rape."

She sniffed. "Maybe, maybe not."

James sighed. "Sophia—"

"What would you have me do?" She inadvertently smacked him in the gut as she brandished her arms. "Abandon him?"

James grunted at the sudden contact. "You can convince Dawson to move into town with you."

She snorted. "He's afraid of strangers. He won't leave the mountains, and I can't desert him."

James growled. "But he can't protect you from the redcoats!"

"He's mad and he's dangerous. The islanders fear him, so he protects me just fine. And the redcoats are too busy hunting Maroons to bother with me again. I'll be fine."

"Damn it, Sophia—"

"I'm home," she said succinctly.

Candlelight shimmered through the unmasked windows. She spied a shadow bobbing inside the ramshackle abode—and stilled.

Despair clutched her heart with its icy fingers. The last vestige of fortitude slipped from her tired soul and she approached the house with flat energy, overwhelmed. Sometimes she still desired to leave her father. Sometimes the fickle feelings still haunted her. But the treacherous moment was always fleeting. She shrugged off the cumbersome shroud of fatigue and grief and entered the house.

Dawson circled the room in an erratic manner, pistol in hand, quarrelling with the shadows, but he quieted as soon as he spotted her.

"Where have you been?"

She sighed. "I needed supplies from town."

"You should have told me."

"I did!" Sophia strutted inside the room and dropped the satchel on the table. "I told you three times!"

He humphed. "Where are the supplies?"

"I didn't get them. I'll have to go into town tomorrow."

"Why?" He eyed her bruises. "What happened to you?" He stared at James, who had entered the house behind her, before he looked at her wounds again.

Dawson lifted his own pistol, aiming it at Black Hawk's head.

Fortunately, James had had the foresight to guess the balmy brigand's thoughts, and had ducked in time, the strident bullet piercing the door instead of his skull.

"He didn't hurt me, Father!" She skirted across the room, her ears ringing from the blast, and wrestled with her parent for the weapon. "It was the redcoats!"

Dawson relinquished the gun and slammed his fist into his palm. "I'll kill them!"

"They're already dead," she snapped, breathless. "Black Hawk killed them."

"Damn it, that's my duty!" He glared at James. "I'm her father."

Slowly James righted himself. "I'm sorry, Dawson."

He humphed again, then set his wild eyes on Sophia. "What's for supper, woman?"

She sighed. She buried her father's pistol inside a copper pot, her head pulsing, her bones aching.

She looked across the room at James, who offered her an encouraging smile, and she wished with all her heart he would stay with her — forever.

CHAPTER 4

We can burst the bonds which chain us,
Which cold human hands have wrought,
And where none shall dare contain us
We can meet again, in thought.

"PARTING" CHARLOTTE BRONTË

James rested on the cool deck of the verandah, his legs stretched and crossed at the ankles. The thick wood beams supporting the awning, supported his back as well. He listened to the distant swell of the water, the beach a few chains away from the abandoned plantation house, and lazily perused the unkempt garden, feral with jungle growth.

"I suppose even pirates need a break from pillaging."

He chuckled at her sharp wit. The blood warmed in his veins. She cut through the ferns and approached the house in an idle manner, her long white dress flirting with the sultry breeze. Sunlight caressed her dark and wavy locks, the thick tresses highlighted with touches of gold.

James's world righted itself as soon as he spotted her. A part of him had still sheltered misgivings about his plan, but now that he was with her again, he was sure he was doing the right thing.

Sophia pulled him towards her with her bewitching brown eyes, and he obeyed her silent, sensual call. He lifted off the front steps.

"Why have you summoned me here, Black Hawk?"

There was a smudge across her tanned cheek, the shadow of a bruise. He stroked the healing wound with the pad of his thumb, blood pounding in his head with rabid rage. He quashed the black memory of the attack with savage regard. He would not let it spoil the intimate moment.

"Was it a summons?" he said gruffly.

She swatted at his distracting fingers, huffing, but he had sensed the wanton shudder that had wracked her bones. He had missed her too. He had suffered the pangs of separation from her for nigh three weeks. The sea had served as his mistress for so long, but now land beckoned to him as well. Sophia beckoned to him.

"The note read: *meet me at the old plantation house.*" She quirked a slender brow. "It sounded like a summons to me."

He smiled. "An invitation."

James girded his muscles as she pressed her belly into his midriff, weaving her fingers through his unruly beard, scratching his cheeks like she was greeting a faithful mutt.

"I don't know if I like the beard. It hides the infamous brigand."

He sighed at her rough touch and bussed the palm of her hand, blood swelling in his veins. "And do you like the infamous brigand?"

She smiled coyly.

"Why have you *invited* me here, Black Hawk?"

She rounded his figure and scaled the front steps, strolling the portico like the lady of the house. She observed the classical structure for a moment: the thick stone walls, the slatted shutters, the shell and coral motif that framed the large wood door and arched windows.

"Do you like the house, Sophia?"

She wrapped her arms around a wide column. The gingerbread fretwork stretched across the length of the verandah, casting her features in playful shadows.

"It's lovely," she said.

"It's mine."

Sophia looked at him, bemused. "What?"

He admired her lanky form in silhouette. She hugged the beam, one with the house. It was constructed to carry her footfalls, to shelter her sleeping head. It was designed to protect her from the elements ... and to offer her freedom.

He joined her under the roof. He folded his arms across his chest and pressed his shoulder against the wood column. "I purchased it this morning."

"It's too big for you."

"I don't intend to live here alone."

Slowly she lifted her eyes, the bronze pools shimmering in the sunlight. "I'm sure you'll be very happy here with your brothers."

"Bite your tongue, woman." He stroked her lush hair. He coiled a long lock around his finger. He was brimming with a dream: a dream of solidarity. "It's your home, too, Sophia."

She munched on her bottom lip, the playful banter no more. "I know."

James sensed the turmoil in her heart. He splayed his fingers and raked his hand through her tresses. He gripped the base of her skull, then separated her from the column. She slipped her arms around his waist instead, and he sighed with satisfaction to feel her limbs curled around his body, embracing him in a sturdy hold. It was quiet inside his soul when he was with her. He ached to keep it that way.

She sighed and buried her features in his bust. "I can't live with you."

He had anticipated the objection. "It's two miles from your father's home. You can prepare his food and see to his needs during the day, every day if you like . . . and then come home to me."

She seemed to struggle with the proposition, the dream. "But he's helpless."

"He's not helpless," said James. "He lived for years without your care, remember? And you'll still be with him for a good portion of each day. He'll grow accustomed to the change."

She was quiet.

"What is it, Sophia?" He bussed the crown of her head. "Do you fear censure from the islanders?"

She snorted. "I don't care what the islanders think of me."

"Then what's wrong?"

"Why are you doing this?" She looked up at him earnestly, seeking truth. "What do you want from me?"

"I want you."

The words welled inside him with fierceness,

resounded in his head. He breathed the words and the meaning they conveyed: he wanted her. He wanted to be with her. He wanted to protect her. There was no other way to describe the profound need he had to return to land.

He brushed her sweet lips with his mouth. "Well?"

"*Irie*," she consented in her native patios.

The garden was brimming with orchids and honeysuckles and ginger lilies, tart fruit trees and sweet spices. A cool sea breeze whisked through the botanical paradise, stirring the flora in animation.

James was at the garden's edge. He eyed the sweeping landscape, rolling with bright bushels of both native and imported species, pulsing with vivid life.

Sophia was nestled amid the floral splendor. A white orchid with a brilliant red centre kissed her ear as she pruned its leaves with tenderness. The blossom reminded him of burning passion buried deep within the soul. A heat soon swelled in his belly, his blood: a comforting heat.

James watched the woman from afar. So lovely. More lovely than any of the delicate blooms. She was kneeling, her bare toes buried in the moist soil. She had pinned he hair in a loose swirl, and draped her limbs in a flowing white shift.

She cared for the garden, for him with such passion. And it welled inside him, the profound and stirring sentiment . . .

She stilled.

She closed her eyes. She had sensed him. She

Mistress of Paradise

waited quietly for him to come and greet her. She beckoned him with her silence.

Slowly he moved away from the trees. He approached her crouching figure. He hunkered behind her, overwhelmed with rampant desire.

Softly he bussed her throat.

I love you, Sophia.

He lifted off his haunches and headed inside the plantation house. He swaggered across the portico, swarming with potted Jamaican Roses. The pink blossoms glowed as the crimson sunlight passed through the translucent petals.

He entered the shady house. The shutters blocked the late afternoon heat. It had taken months to restore the building. There were white-washed walls and dark, cedar wood beams in the ceilings. Long and wispy drapes adorned the arched windows. The airy space was filled with the potent scent of freshly cooked fare, and James breathed deep, absorbing the sights and aromas, the essence of home.

"Are you hungry?"

She had followed him inside the house. He watched her as she wiped her slender, grimy fingers in her skirt, smearing the dirt across the white fabric.

"Aye," he said gruffly.

She smirked. "I'm not on the menu." She strutted through the great hall with a sensual grace before she entered the back kitchen. "I'm making roast beef with red beans and yams."

James admired her curvy figure from the door as she moved about the renovated enclosure, gathering pewter cups and plates, preparing the table for the evening meal. The stone floor maintained a cool temperature inside the room. Pots and pans dangled from the ceiling. There were even dry spices bundled together and hooked on the wall.

Sophia next stirred the beans, simmering in a copper pot on the great iron stove. He enjoyed observing her as she tended to the household chores. It was a simple pleasure that inspired quiet reflections.

"Where have you been?" she wondered.

"I sneaked into town as Captain Hawkins." He removed a small, glittering item from his pocket. "I have something for you."

She glanced at him askance. "What is it?"

He approached the stove, the heat from the wide iron belly warming his cheeks. He presented her with the short boot knife, bejeweled handle and leather sheath.

"I'm going to teach you how to use it," he said. "I want you to know how to protect yourself with a blade."

She fingered the weapon. "It's so small."

He lifted a sardonic brow at the double-entendre. "It's three inches long and double edged. It's very deadly if you know how to wield it. It's also slim enough to fit anywhere on your body . . ."

She slipped the blade and sheath between her ample breasts.

He grunted. "Like there."

Sophia offered him a smoky smile. "Thank you, Black Hawk."

A deep and pressing hunger gripped his bones, filled his soul. He lost every desire for roast beef and yams and slipped his fingers through Sophia's thick hair, drawing her into his arms for a sensuous kiss.

"Oh, am I interrupting?" Quincy staggered inside the kitchen. "Good." He simpered. "Hullo, So-fee-a."

Sophia chuckled at the scamp's maladroit flirtation.

James snarled at the interruption.

"Good evening, Quincy." She parted from James and illuminated an oil lamp. "Have you come for supper?"

"Don't encourage him to stay, sweetheart." James glowered at the woozy pup in the superior light. "Are you drunk?"

He hiccupped. "No."

James sighed.

Quincy dropped into a chair and propped his feet on the table. "I have news."

"What news?"

Quincy grinned. "I'm a man."

James balked. "Blimey!"

Sophia hooted with laughter as she mashed the boiled yams.

Blood pounded in James's veins and pumped into his head, washing away the last vestige of tranquility, making him blind with vertigo.

"You're thirteen!" he stormed.

"So?" said Quincy. "How old were you when you first bedded a woman?"

"Aye, Black Hawk." There was a sassy gleam in Sophia's eyes. "How old were you?"

He growled, "Not thirteen."

The witch had a foul sense of humor, he thought darkly. The matter wasn't droll. Quincy was far too young to be chasing after skirts.

He glared at the boy. "Do you even know what to do?"

"Of course, I do."

The pup sounded indignant.

James rubbed his brow, smarting. Thoughts teemed in his head. What was the ass thinking? He was so naïve and inexperienced. He wasn't even prepared for the consequences. He might end up with the pox if he rutted with a tart. Did he know to look for the signs: the sores, the rash on the palms?

James took in a deep breath. He had anticipated Quincy's inauguration into "manhood," but not for a few more years. He had believed he'd have more time to educate the boy in the matters of sex. Bloody hell!

"Where the devil is Will? Eddie?"

The pup shrugged. "I dunno."

"At least we know why he's foxed." Sophia poured James a glass of white rum to calm him. "He needed the encouragement."

James downed the fiery liquid in one hearty swig. It blessedly burned his belly and torched his riled senses.

He looked back at Quincy. "Who did you bed?"

The boy grinned. "A sea nymph."

"A fish?"

Hope sprouted in James's breast. Perhaps the reckless fledging hadn't lost his virginity after all. He had tipped the bottle, true. However, he might have floundered with the doxy and ended up on the beach in bed with the "fishes."

"She's not a fish," Quincy protested.

"There's the manatees along the coast." Sophia served the bowls of yams and strained beans. "Sailors have mistaken them for mermaids for years."

"She's *not* a fish," the pup insisted. "She came from the water, tall and beautiful with the biggest set of . . ."

James sensed the muscles twitching in his cheek. He wanted to smash something . . . like Quincy head. He slammed the empty glass on the table instead.

The pup wasn't perturbed, though. He sighed wistfully instead. "It was perfect."

Sophia chortled.

Quincy reached across the table and grabbed an ackee from a wood bowl. "Hmm . . . that looks good."

"No!" James shouted.

Sophia scuttled across the room and grabbed the fruit from his fingers. "That's poisonous!"

Quincy paled. "Then what's it doing on the table?"

"Seasoning." She chastised, "You can eat it *only* when it's ripe." She set the roast beef in front of him. "Eat this instead. On second thought, I think it's time I put you to bed."

She dragged him out of the chair and escorted him through the kitchen and toward the guest quarters on the second level.

"Be careful, Sophia," James said dryly. He raked his fingers roughly through his hair, uprooting pieces. "He's a man now."

Quincy puckered his lips. "Aye, a virile man."

Sophia pinched the boy's neck, curtailing his clumsy seduction, and steered him up the narrow servant steps at the back of the room. "I'll remember that."

James dropped into a seat and lowered his

throbbing brow into his cupped hands. Where the hell were the rest of his brothers? Why weren't they looking after the boy? Did James have to manage *every* blasted moment of their lives?

A few taxing minutes later, a set of comforting hands slipped over his shoulders and caressed his pectorals.

"You shouldn't fret." She bussed the back of his head. "The pup's fine."

The woman's touch was like balm. It soothed the demons ranting in his head. "Is the boy asleep?"

"Aye."

She circled the chair. James opened his arms and welcomed her into his lap with a deep, delightful sigh. He embraced her waist and buried his face in the crook between her neck and shoulder.

"Quincy talks in his sleep." She stroked his beard. "Like you."

He frowned. "I don't talk in my sleep."

"You snore. It's likewise as irritating."

James humphed. He closed his eyes and allowed the woman's sweet touch to lull his nettled senses. The storm in his breast quieted. He listened to Sophia's rhythmic breathing, deep and steady. He sensed her pulse against his palm as he fingered her throat. He absorbed the tart scent of citrus soap on her skin, let the sweet smell invade his lungs and stifle his sour temperament.

"I like your family."

"Are you mad, woman?"

She chuckled: a wicked and smoky sound that aroused his carnal impulses. "They don't judge me for being Dawson's daughter."

"How is your father?"

"He's fine." Sophia scratched his cheek. She sharpened her claws on his scruffy facial hair. "You were right. He's grown accustomed to my daily visits and evening departures. He still rants he's going to shoot you for taking me away from him. But he won't do it. I think he knows I'm happy here with you."

James cupped her hip and rubbed her arse in a provocative manner. The woman's words offered him great pleasure. In truth, he desired her contentment above all else . . . but the direction in which their talk was moving had him bristling, for there was one thing he could never give her.

"I don't want to marry, Sophia."

"I know." She sighed. "Pirates don't marry."

"It has nothing to do with being a pirate."

James closed his eyes as a dark memory raided the harmony in his soul: a woman's haunting sobs.

You must help me, James. You must help me now that Papa is gone. I need you, James. I can't take care of you and William by myself. You will help Mama, won't you, James?

Even as a child he had possessed an overwhelming duty to protect his family . . . but he had failed. His mother had suffered from poverty and loneliness for years. She had depended on him for help for the twelve years his father had been at sea, and he had failed her.

James shuddered at the macabre reflection. He would not create another family. He would not forge a wedded bond with Sophia and let her depend on him for all her needs . . . and then be disappointed. He already had one rambunctious family to look after.

"It's called wed*lock* for a reason," he said. "It isn't right to cage two wild birds. Are you all right with that, Sophia?"

She shrugged. "I don't care about convention."

Nay, she didn't care about convention. He admired that trait about her. The woman had strength, wits, and will. She had the wherewithal to take care of herself and the means to want for nothing should he perish in a foray at sea. She didn't need him . . . but she wanted him.

"You're stiff, Black Hawk."

"Am I?" he said hoarsely.

She nipped his ear. "I mean, your muscles. Are you still upset about Quincy?" She bussed his lips. "I can make you forget about your troubles."

He shuddered deep in his bones. "Aye." He groaned as she nuzzled his mouth and twisted her fingers in his hair. "Make me forget, sweetheart."

Sophia straddled him. She wrapped her arms around him, trapping him. It was a blessed prison. He took in every part of her: every touch, taste, and scent. Filled with the woman's essence, her spirit, there was no room inside his soul for unrest.

He clinched her waist.

"Oh, no," she said in a sultry whisper. "I take command tonight."

James hardened, expression dark.

"No," he said brusquely.

She chuckled: a throaty sound. "Shall I fetch the chess board? Loser pays a forfeit."

"I don't want to play chess *now*."

She licked her lips in a teasing gesture, unabashed.

"Then forgo the game and just pay the forfeit."

James gnashed his teeth. The game had become their means of settling a dispute. It offered the winner absolute right—and the loser absolute surrender—in the contested matter. But James wasn't too keen on the proposal. He was always the dominant one in bed. She liked it that way too. Game, be damned! He needed the woman now.

He lifted her skirt and rubbed his hands across her soft thighs, feeling her carnal shivers—but she grabbed his wrists and tsked. "We do this my way."

He had once said the very same words to her—and it was beyond irritating to hear the expression echoed back to him. He positioned her quim snuggly over his erection. "You would make me wait, woman?"

She sighed in sensual hunger. Her obvious need for him made him even harder in return. He thought to disabuse her of the balmy demand to be in control, to tempt her to submit to his will and be done with the inconvenient matter of the game—but she was headstrong.

"I take the lead . . . or we play to settle the matter. Perhaps you win and get your way. Or perhaps you lose and I get mine." She shrugged. "Either way, we waste time."

Blood surged in his veins, making his heart pound like canon blasts.

"Fine," he growled. "Do it your way."

She offered him a wicked smile. "Trust me, James. You need to let go. It will do you good."

"Horseshit."

She winked. She lifted off his lap. He ached in his

belly for her return. He watched her sharply as she crossed the room and retrieved the cord she used to fasten the herbs and spices. She snipped a long piece from the roll with the iron shears.

"What are you doing?" he demanded.

She circled the chair again. "Give me your hands."

James stiffened. Phantom fingers squeezed his ribs and crushed his lungs. It went against his every instinct: submission. He was always in command. He was always in charge of his ship, his crew. He maintained his wits—and his hands—at all times. The very thought of giving up control made him sweat, stirred his heartbeat to pulsing life.

"Put your hands behind your back, James."

"No."

He lifted from the chair, restless.

She placed her palms on his rigid shoulders and guided him back into the seat. "Pay the forfeit."

Blood throbbed in his skull. He struggled against the profound sentiment that he was drowning. "I can't."

"Yes, you can." She took his hands and steered them behind the chair. "Trust me, James."

He was breathing hard, his muscles moist with sweat, as she firmly looped the cord around his wrists, securing him to the chair.

James flexed his arms, but the bond was tight: a seaman's knot. He instantly regretted submitting to her request. He thought about breaking the chair. He was daft. He had *let* the woman tie him to the furniture. It wasn't right. He needed to get loose. He needed to take her on the table—now.

"That's better." She rucked her skirt and straddled him again. "Relax, James."

"Untie me."

She let out a smoky chortle as she removed the pins from her hair. The long locks rained across her bust in glorious waves, the shimmering lamplight reflecting off the glossy tresses, bewitching him.

She combed her fingers through his bushy beard. "I won't hurt you."

James struggled against the cord, his wrists chafed. "Next time I win a forfeit, I'm going to tie you to our bed and make you scream."

"Promise?"

He grunted. "You vicious —"

She curtailed the threat with a smoldering kiss that drained the breath from his lungs and the fight from his blood.

Sophia.

He pleaded in his soul.

She gripped the open collar at his shirt and rent the garment. She splayed her fingers and pressed her hot palms against his chest, branding his flesh.

James sucked in a deep breath. He sensed the world was crumbling under his feet. He needed to take back control. He needed to bed the woman, to feed her sensual hunger. He was a worthless man when restrained. And the more she moaned, the more he jerked his arms, frantic to break the knots.

She scraped her fingernails across his firm muscles, begging him for more. *Let me go!* he screamed in his head. He would give her everything she desired, then. But the witch tortured him instead. She reached between her legs and groped for the buttons of his trousers.

"I want you." She undulated her hips. "I want you so much, James."

The wood splintered as he wrenched his arms. He ached in his bones for freedom, for power.

Sophia slipped her hands inside his trousers and stroked his thick erection. "I need you inside me." She bussed his lips. "Deep inside me."

He groaned in agony: a dark and feral noise. "If you don't release me, I'll—"

She sucked his bottom lip, raked it between her teeth. "Are you still fighting for control?" She lifted her rump and eased her wet quim over his erection. "I have control, James."

He closed his eyes and gasped at the slick feel of her muscles clinching his stiff cock. His body raged with restless energy. He wanted to rut. He thrust his hips in an aggressive attempt to take command, but she maintained control. She refused to move with him.

"Be still," she whispered in a throaty vein. "Let me take you."

He girded his muscles in protest. He was supposed to take her. He was supposed to fill her. *Him!* It wasn't right. He wasn't supposed to sit there like a lazy sod.

"Let go, James." She moved her body over him in waves. "Trust me."

He shuddered in defeat.

Sophia bucked her hips in steady movements. "That's it." She whimpered. Sweat glistened across her brow and bust. "That's it, James."

Blood thumped inside his head with wicked force

as he let the woman ravish him, let every last defiant instinct drain from his body.

"Yes!" she cried.

Her wanton, guttural sounds gratified him. He stopped struggling with her. He joined her in the erotic dance. If she bore down on him, he raised his hips to give her more. If she searched for his lips, he offered her his mouth and tongue.

Take me, sweetheart.

James groaned in avid hunger, wet with sweat. The friction from their heated coupling burned his blood. His heart was pounding. He gasped for breath as the tension in his cock tightened even more, and he ached for sweet release . . . for sweet surrender.

The rhythmic pounding obscured all his other senses. He cried out as a deep explosion rocked his body, blessed relief spreading to every stressed muscle and nerve. He poured his hot seed into her womb. And she took in every drop, sapping him of strength.

James shuddered and dropped his head back against the chair, searching for precious breath. All was quiet inside his soul. He reveled in the stillness.

"Was that so hard, Black Hawk?"

He choked on his laughter. He was brimming with warmth and sated delight. "Aye, it was bloody hard." He buried his face in her throat and bussed her throbbing pulse. "Now untie me, witch."

She sighed. "The idea of 'letting go' didn't last too long, did it?"

"Untie me. Now." He said in a more husky voice, "I want to give you what you've given me."

She smiled. "Well, in that case . . ."

CHAPTER 5

So there's no use in weeping,
Bear a cheerful spirit still;
Never doubt that Fate is keeping
Future good for present ill!

"PARTING" CHARLOTTE BRONTË

Sophia travelled through the cobblestone street with a basket of food in her arms. The wide thoroughfare was flanked by colonial-style structures with mustard-yellow facades and green, sun-bleached roof shingles. Fronted with white columns and second-story balustrades, the uniform buildings encapsulated rigid British rule.

Sophia passed under the massive Union Jack flag positioned beside the courthouse entrance. She had spent most of the day in town, gathering ingredients for the evening meal. She wanted to prepare a memorable supper for James, for it was one year ago today that she had first met him.

A cool sea breeze bustled through Harbour Street, twisting her loose hair. She spied the wanted posters along the courthouse wall and smiled at the exorbitant, one hundred pound reward offered for Black Hawk's head. The infamous pirate had changed her life in so many wondrous ways. She had settled into a comfortable, even complete existence with the man. And to celebrate their anniversary, she wanted to prepare his favorite repast: coco bread, ginger chicken and rum cake for dessert. She just had to buy the wine.

As she approached the tavern, the impudent whistles made her bristle. She ignored the tramps, loitering outside the establishment. She was accustomed to their jeers and heckles whenever she ventured into town for supplies. It was common knowledge that she was Captain James Hawkins mistress, and she disregarded the vagrants as she entered the pub.

Sophia purchased the red wine from the barkeep. She nestled the bottle inside her basket, then departed the public house and resumed her steady march home.

"Give us a kiss, Sophia!"

One drunkard grabbed his cock in a crude gesture and sucked on his bottom lip, making a loud smacking sound. "Kiss me, Sophia. I'm tastier."

"No, kiss me! I've got a prick you can ride all night."

Sophia dropped the basket, blistering heat coursing through her veins. She was about to draw her knife and cut off the foul men's cods, when the three hecklers quickly composed their mocking brows and sneering lips.

A young woman approached the rabble. She was pale, curly locks a fashionable flaxen blonde. She looked ridiculous in the tropical heat with her layers of linen, a bonnet and parasol to match. Sophia could see the sweat glistening across her wide brow and slim, aquiline nose. However, she maintained the regalia with a chaperone to boot . . . and she commanded respect.

The governor's wife strolled past the vagrants.

"Good day, Mrs. Smith," the men murmured in unison and doffed their scruffy caps.

Mrs. Smith ignored the tramps. She walked past them with formal grace, offering Sophia a brief look of scorn as she went.

Sophia fisted her palms, staring after the prim and proper woman. Her heart thundered in her ears, her mind swelled with dark thoughts as shame billowed inside her breast. She struggled to tamp the roiling grief—the rage!—blustering in her head.

Mrs. Smith condemned her as a whore and treated her accordingly. The islanders' snickers and sneers had become commonplace, for Sophia was considered a trollop: no one of consequence, no one deserving respect.

The hecklers started up again, their jeers growing louder in her head. Sophia grabbed the basket and hurried through the lively street.

In an hour, she was home. She stormed the plantation house and dumped the basket of food on the kitchen table, the ingredients rolling across the polished wood surface.

James entered the room and grabbed an onion before it hit the floor. "Is something the matter, sweetheart?"

She glared at him, sweating, pulses rapping in her ears. The quick and hardy hike home hadn't cooled her thoughts or numbed her throbbing senses.

The taunts and crude remarks still resounded in her head. She had had enough of the ridicule.

Quietly she climbed the staircase and retrieved the chessboard from their bedroom. She returned to the kitchen and cleared the table before she arranged the players across the checkered playing surface.

James studied her curt, efficient movements. He raised a black brow. "Care to enlighten me about the dispute?"

She was mum. The derision, the looks of disdain still swirled inside her head. She trembled with mortification and battled the mawkish impulse to weep.

Sophia snagged a seat. With energy, she smacked the ivory pawn against the board, making the first move.

James watched her with a baffled look in his deep blue eyes, but he assumed the opposite chair and moved a jade player forward.

As the strenuous match culminated to a victorious end, she stiffly proclaimed, "Checkmate."

James reclined in the chair and folded his thick arms across his strapping chest. "You win, sweetheart. Ask anything of me you wish."

"Marry me."

The man's expression darkened. "What?"

Sophia skull throbbed with hurtful snipes and spurned regards. There was only one way to silence the slights and avoid the snubs: marriage. As the captain's wife, she would command respect. She wouldn't have to confront the mockery every time she ventured into town. She wouldn't have to suffer the shame and ignominy every time she gathered in polite society. Her life with James would remain the same. She already shared a home, a bed with the man. A wedding wouldn't upset the intimate bond or the routine that they both cherished. It would simply root out the last distasteful hindrance preventing them from being truly happy.

"Marry me, James."

"No."

The brusque response shattered her equanimity. He glared at her like a disobedient tar, and she sensed a foul sentiment stirring deep in her belly.

He was content with their affair. He was comfortable having her as his whore. It was *she* who was unhappy, not James. He cared nothing for the islanders' whispers or hateful chortles. He cared nothing for her. Not really. He cared for her body. He cared for her cooking. But he cared nothing for her heart. Otherwise, he would not have refused the challenge loss. He had *never* refused a challenge loss in the past. He was too honorable to go back on his word … but then she had never asked him to be her husband.

A cold darkness filled her soul and she sprinted from the kitchen, making her way into their bedroom. She let out the sob pressing on her lung: one mournful wail. She then swallowed the rest of her tears … and let the darkness flow through her heart.

She scanned the space, the intimate haven. She spied the great, four-poster bed draped in soft white sheets. The bedding was still rumpled. She had left early in the morning to fetch the ingredients for the evening meal. James had remained behind, sleeping. She parted the canopy veil and looked at the lumpy feather tick and puckered linens, heart aching.

It was all a lie: every soulful touch and whispered word. He had charmed her, lured her into his bed to keep it warm.

Whore!

The redcoats had been right. She was nothing but a willing wench.

Sophia stiffened as firm, robust fingers cupped her arms and a warm wall of muscle pressed into her backside.

"Let's not fight, sweetheart."

She took in a heavy breath through her nose as he fingered her long locks and exposed her throat, bussing her neck, her pounding pulse.

She closed her eyes, quivering. He had tricked her. He had shammed her into thinking she was more to him than just a mistress. Even now he bewitched her senses with his soft caresses and sultry kisses.

"I go to sea tomorrow." He slipped his arms around her waist and rocked his hips in a sensual dance. "I don't want to quarrel with you, Sophia. Not today of all days."

"Why not today?" she demanded. "Because it's our anniversary?"

Was he going to feign interest in the affair? Was he going to pretend it mattered to him . . . like it had mattered to her?

"Yes it's our anniversary," he said softly, thrusting his pelvis in step to the imaginary music. "Is that why you asked me to marry you?"

She snorted. He believed her too emotional because it was their anniversary. But she wasn't suffering from sentimentality. She was suffering from shame. The islanders considered her a trollop. Did James too? She decided to find out.

"When will you take me to England, James?"

"Why do you want to go to England?"

She lilted with him in the quiet room. "I want to see your homeland. I want to meet your sister. You've said so much about her. I think it's time I make her acquaintance."

She waited, breathless, as the moments passed.

"It's too cold in England," he said at last. "You need the hot sun, sweetheart. It's better for you here on the island. Besides, who would look after your father?"

She released the breath she was holding at the man's hedging response. He would not marry her. He would not introduce her to his beloved sister. He had had no qualms about introducing her to his brothers, but he would not acquaint her, a wench, with his saintly sister.

He was ashamed of her.

Sophia let the man's artful thrusts hush her nettled senses. She would dance with the heartless brigand . . . one last time.

James cut through the tepid seawater and mounted the sandy shore. He eyed the plantation house poised proud on the hilltop. There was a candle burning in one of the bedroom windows.

"I'm coming, Sophia."

He was filled with a savage hunger . . . for her. After a thrilling raid at sea, blood pulsed through his veins. He wanted to prolong the pleasurable rush of energy, to kiss every bit of her soft flesh before he buried himself deep within her.

In quick strides he moved across the beach and through the wild bush. Palms scratched his naked torso, and he swatted the foliage, startling the parakeets, who, squawking, took to flight.

The narrow footpath broadened as he approached the house with its thick stone walls, two feet dense. So sturdy. So cool. The limestone mortar that covered the exterior gleamed in the moonlight like white gold. Brilliant coral framed the large wood door and the arched windows.

James stepped into the lush garden filled with fireflies, orchids and fruit trees. He snapped a star apple from a sagging branch and bit into the tangy skin.

But nothing compared to the sweet taste of her.

Inside the house the cedar floorboards were cool against his bare feet. He climbed the dark staircase two steps at a time and moved through the airy passageway, heading for the familiar door.

He was dressed only in trousers, sheared at the knees, ready for a quick disrobe. He opened the door with great expectation—but inside the large canopy bed with white cotton sheets was empty.

"Sophia?"

James spied the *Bonny Meg* veiled with moonbeams and anchored a league away through the open window. She was privy to his return; she could see the ship clearly. So why wasn't she waiting for him?

A balmy breeze tickled the candle flame sitting on the sill. The flickering glow illuminated a small box.

In irritation he stepped across the room, and tossed the pit of the star apple out the window before he picked up the curious carton. With disregard for the plain packaging, he ripped apart the paper.

A fob watch.

James lifted the timepiece to better inspect the splendid craftsmanship and sighted the elegant inscription on the back:

MAY YOU ROT IN EVERLASTING HELL

He gripped the cold gold between his fingers, knuckles white. The blood pulsing through his veins now pounded in his ears. He let out a robust cry before he smashed the watch against the wall.

The glass face shattered, the hands stopped ticking.

He stormed from the room, the plantation house, and hiked in bold strides along the dark and narrow path leading to Dawson's hut.

James didn't care if he sliced his bare feet across sharp rocks or jagged roots. He didn't care about anything—except finding Sophia.

He reached the ramshackle structure. It was dark. Eerily dark. And quiet. No familiar ranting. He stepped inside the abode, his heart throbbing, his limbs sweating after the hardy journey through the moonlit mountain, and found the room empty, filled with shadows.

His heart dropped, sunk right into his belly. He clutched the door as he searched the dim space with his eyes for any hint of her whereabouts, but it was in vain. She had left behind no clues. He had been at sea for weeks, and she had had plenty of time to pack up her father, her gold — everything that she cared about — and desert him.

James slammed the door closed and returned to the plantation house, to their bedroom. But the once intimate haven offered him no comfort now. It was nothing but a gloomy shell without Sophia's presence.

The leaves rustled outside the opened window, and he spotted a serpent coiled around a branch: a Jamaican yellow boa. He glared at the snake, thinking about his venomous lover. He then glared at the damaged timepiece still on the ground, imagined grinding the cursed watch into the floorboards … but he crouched beside it instead and started to pick up the pieces.

It was the only gift she had ever given him, however foul her sense of humor. And now that she had left him, it was the only keepsake he had of her.

To find out if Sophia and James find love in each other's arms again, read their story in *The Infamous Rogue*, available now from Avon Books.

ABOUT THE AUTHOR

ALEXANDRA BENEDICT is the author of several historical romance novels. Her work has received critical acclaim from *Booklist* and a rare and coveted starred review from *Publishers Weekly*. *Romantic Times* awarded her a "Top Pick" review and raved: "There is nothing quite as exciting as finding a fresh, vibrant new voice, and Benedict has it!" All of Alexandra's books are translated into various languages. To learn more visit: www.AlexandraBenedict.ca

Alexandra also writes young adult fantasy fiction with a romantic twist under the pen name ALEX BENEDICT. Don't miss her debut novel SO DOWN I FALL: a dark re-imagining of THE LITTLE MERMAID. Visit www.AlexBenedict.ca for more detail.

Made in the USA
Middletown, DE
15 March 2018